ARTHUR TRICKS THE TOOTH FAIRY

牙仙来过了

（美）马克·布朗　绘著

范晓星　译

CHISO 新疆青少年出版社

Arthur ran to the breakfast table.

"Look, D.W.," he said.

Arthur waved a dollar.

"The Tooth Fairy left it

under my pillow."

"Why?" asked D.W.
"She takes baby teeth
and leaves money,"
Arthur said.

3

"That's goofy," said D.W.

"What does she do

with all those old teeth?"

Arthur thought.

"Maybe her castle is made

of teeth," he said.

"Where does she get the money?"

asked D.W.

"You ask too many questions,"

said Arthur.

The next morning

D.W. ran to the breakfast table.

"My tooth is loose!" she shouted.

"It is not," Arthur said.

"Is too," said D.W.

"Nope. You are too young

 to lose teeth," said Arthur.

"Not fair!" said D.W.

When Arthur got home from school,

the house was very noisy.

Slam!SLAM!SLAM!

went D.W.'s door.

"What are you doing?"

shouted Arthur.

"Pulling out my loose tooth,"

said D.W.

"Oh, no! Stop it!" said Arthur.

"Your tooth is NOT loose."

8

9

That night D.W. said,

"I have a toothache.

My tooth needs to be pulled out."

"Mom, she's making it up,"

said Arthur.

"Am not," said D.W.

"It really hurts."

"If it still hurts tomorrow,

we'll visit the dentist

on our way to the museum,"

said their mother.

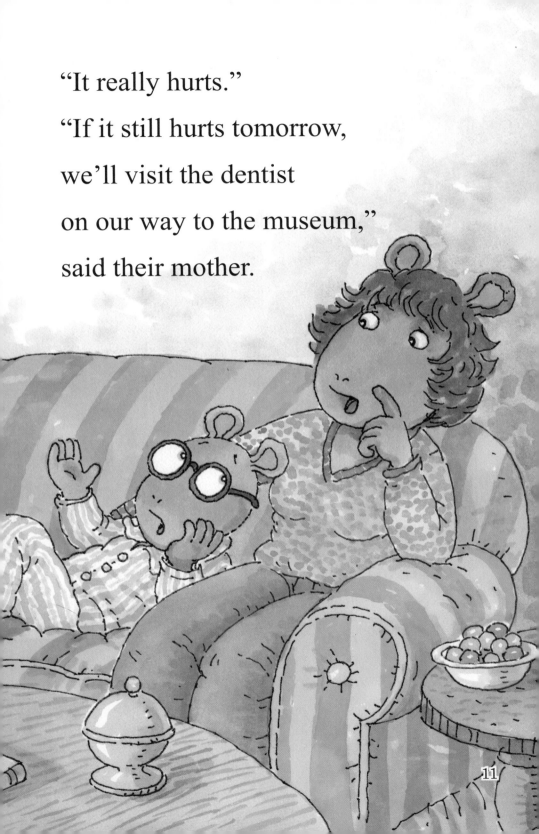

The next day they went
to the dentist.
D.W. jumped into his chair.
"Your teeth are perfect,"
said the dentist. "I don't think
the Tooth Fairy will visit you
for a year or two."
"See, I told you," said Arthur.
"No one believes me," cried D.W.

13

D.W. dragged her feet
all the way to the museum.
Everywhere she looked
she saw teeth.
Dinosaur teeth.

14

Shark teeth.

Tiger teeth.

D.W. could not stop thinking
about teeth.

At the museum shop
their mother said,
"You can each buy
one little thing."
Arthur looked
at everything.

But D.W. knew just what
she wanted.
"I'm going to buy
a shark's tooth," she said.
"I have a great idea!"

17

That night D.W. couldn't wait
to go to bed.
"I'll tell you a secret, Arthur,
if you promise not to tell
Mom and Dad," said D.W.
"Promise," said Arthur.
"The Tooth Fairy
is coming tonight.
I'm going to trick her
with my shark's tooth,"
said D.W.
"It's really going to work."
"I sure hope so," said Arthur.
"Because I'm tired of hearing
about teeth."

That night D.W. dreamed
about the Tooth Fairy.

And that night Arthur decided
that the Tooth Fairy
needed a little help.

Before the sun was up,

D.W. ran into Arthur's room.

"Look! Look what the Tooth Fairy

left me!" she shouted.

Arthur opened his eyes.

"I tricked the Tooth Fairy!
I tricked the Tooth Fairy!"
sang D.W.
"I did it. I really did!"

"And tonight I'm going

to do it again!" shouted D.W.

译文

2. 亚瑟跑到餐桌前，手里挥舞着一块钱对朵拉说："朵拉，你看！这是小牙仙留在我枕头底下的！"

3. "为什么呀？"朵拉问。

"因为小牙仙专门爱拿走小孩儿掉的牙齿，然后留下一点钱。"亚瑟回答。

4. "好奇怪哟！"朵拉说，"她拿走那么多牙齿做什么呢？"

亚瑟想了想回答："也许她的城堡就是用牙齿盖起来的。"

"那她怎么有那么多钱呢？"朵拉又问。

"你的问题太多啦！"亚瑟回应道。

6. 第二天早晨，朵拉跑到餐桌前嚷嚷说："我的牙齿也松了！"

"骗人。"亚瑟回答。

7. "真的！"朵拉又嚷。

"不可能，你这么小，还没开始换牙呢。"亚瑟说。

"不公平！"朵拉嘟囔。

8. 亚瑟放学回到家，家里闹哄哄的。

咣当！咣当！咣当！朵拉房间的门咣当乱响。

"你干什么呢？"亚瑟问。

"我在拔牙呀！"朵拉回答。

"快停下！"亚瑟大声喊，"你的牙没有松啊！"

10. 晚上，朵拉小声哼唧："我牙疼，我要拔牙。"

"妈妈，她瞎编呢。"亚瑟说。

"我没有！"朵拉大声喊。

11. "我真的牙疼。"

"要是明天你的牙还疼，我们去博物馆之前，先去看看牙医吧。"妈妈回应。

12. 第二天，他们来到牙医诊所，朵拉一蹦跳上诊椅。

"你的牙齿很好，"牙医伯伯说，"小牙仙这一两年都不会来找你。"

"看看，我都告诉你了吧？"亚瑟说。

"哼，谁都不相信我！"朵拉气得要哭了。

14. 朵拉很不情愿地去参观博物馆。

每到一个地方，她都只看见牙齿：

恐龙的牙齿，

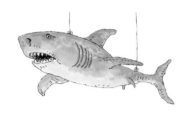

15. <u>鲨鱼的牙齿</u>，
老虎的牙齿……
朵拉满脑子都在想着牙齿的事。

16. 在博物馆的纪念品店里，妈妈说："你们每人可以买一样小东西。"
亚瑟把所有的小纪念品都看了一遍。

17. 朵拉已经很清楚自己想要什么了，她说："我要买一颗<u>鲨鱼的牙齿</u>，
我想到了一个好主意！"

18. 晚上，朵拉急急忙忙地爬上床，对亚瑟说：

"哥哥，告诉你一个秘密，你要保证不告诉爸爸妈妈哦？"

"我保证！"亚瑟回应。

"小牙仙今天晚上会来，我要用这颗鲨鱼的牙齿骗骗她，"朵拉说，"一定会成功的。"

"但愿吧，"亚瑟回答，"我已经听烦了和牙齿有关的事！"

20. 入睡后，朵拉梦见了小牙仙。

21. 亚瑟决定先给小牙仙帮个小忙再睡觉。

22. 太阳还没出来，朵拉就跑进亚瑟的房间大声嚷嚷：

"嘿！快看小牙仙给我留下什么啦！"

亚瑟睁开眼睛。

23. "我让小牙仙上当啦！我让小牙仙上当啦！"朵拉高兴地唱起来，"我成功了，我成功了！"

24. "今天晚上我要再玩一遍！"朵拉快活地喊。

31